Moonshadow
and the
Baby Ice Dragon

GW00809036

Angela James

Other books by Angela James

The Amshir Legacy (a trilogy) for ages 9+

Book 1 The Golden Moonbeam
Book 2 The Theft of the Black Diamond

***

How to Turn a Genie into a Genius in One Move!

A Beginner's Guide to Creative Writing for Kids
(and Parents!)
This is a FREE 45-page educational guide,
available only from Angela's website

'Angela's website details can be found at the back of the book'

In memory of
My Dad

To
Cara

Enjoy the
magic of faeries

Angela James

Contents

Moonshadow and the Baby Ice Dragon

Chapter 1

Moonshadow is a woodland fairy, but a fairy who doesn't like rules. She loves drinking fresh dew from an acorn cup, but *not* the washing up afterwards. She likes picking juicy blackberries from the hedgerows, but

not cleaning the purple stains from her hands. Her pixie boots are often muddy, and filled with water from playing leapfrog with the frogs around the woodland pond; and as for going to bed at sunset – that is a rule for the other woodland fairy folk, but *not* for Moonshadow.

'The woodland is dangerous at night,' her best friend, Willow, warned her. 'There are owls looking for a tasty snack, and

witches only too willing to capture a fairy and steal her magic.'

'Pooh!' said Moonshadow. 'I'm not afraid!'

So Moonshadow didn't take any notice. Why should she? After all, she was born in the shadow of a full moon on a summer solstice. Every month, when the moon was full, she would stay awake all night to play in the silvery light. Had any of the other fairies seen the woodland pond looking like a mirror when the moonlight shone on it? Did they know that the moon made the leaves on the trees look like silver coins that shimmered whenever a breeze whispered over them? No, of course not!

They were always tucked up in their beds that they made with ferns and flower petals. But it was a night when the moon

was full and Moonshadow was playing in the silvery light that her adventure began.

Chapter 2

After a long, hot day, Moonshadow had not gone to bed at sunset like the other fairy folk. Instead, she was gazing at the moon's reflection in the woodland pond. A soft breeze stirred the trees and their branches glowed in the moonlight. All of a sudden, a shadow crossed in front of the moon. Moonshadow looked up just as a bat swooped over the pond. It was the largest bat she had ever seen. It was circling overhead, as if looking for something. It was also carrying a large, creamy, oval object.

'I'm over here,' snapped a loud, cackly voice.

The voice was so near to Moonshadow, it made her jump. She quickly hid in the reeds, where she watched and listened, unseen.

'Did you get it?' asked the cackly voice. The bat fluttered overhead and squeaked,

'Yes, mistress, but it's very heavy and I'm so tired!'

'Give it to me then it won't be heavy anymore,' said the voice.

The moonlight was so bright that when a hook-nosed witch stepped out of the bushes, Moonshadow could see her quite clearly. It was Grimella, and she liked catching fairies!

Suddenly, there was a rustling of leaves and twigs, and someone else spoke.

'Evening Grimella,' said a deep voice.

The witch turned around to face a wizard, 'Oh, it's you, Bogwart. What are you doing here?' she asked grumpily.

'I'm here because of something I've heard,' Bogwart replied.

Grimella scowled at him. He was an interfering wizard who couldn't mind his own business.

'And what have you heard?'

Bogwart drew nearer to the witch. Moonshadow could see the wizard's pointy hat; it was taller than Grimella's.

'That you are going to steal a dragon's egg,' he said, 'and I wanted to see if it was true.'

'Why would I want to steal a dragon's egg?' asked Grimella.

'Hmm, now, let me think!' said Bogwart, with a sniff of disapproval. 'If you had a dragon's egg, you would use it for making powerful spells and potions. If the other witches and wizards got to hear about it, they would be angry because it's, well, it's…'

'Yes, it's what?' snapped Grimella.

'It's cheating,' Bogwart snapped back.

Grimella hissed at Bogwart. The bat was still flying around, but it was getting lower and lower to the pond. Then, there was a loud splash. Moonshadow watched the ripples spread out over the water. The bat rose up into the air, but now, it wasn't carrying anything. Grimella snarled at Bogwart.

'Now look what's happened! My bat has dropped the dragon's egg in the pond! If you hadn't been here to interfere, my bat would have given me the egg before it was too tired to carry it anymore.'

Bogwart sneered. 'So it was true! Well, you can't cheat anymore now you've lost the egg, can you?'

Grimella flung her cloak around her shoulders and marched off. Her bat followed, as leaves swirled up from behind her cloak.

Bogwart waited until Grimella was out of sight then he rustled his way back through the bushes in the opposite direction.

Chapter 3

Moonshadow waited until everything was quiet once more. The water in the pond had settled quickly, which made it difficult to know the exact spot where the egg had dropped. After looking around to make sure both Bogwart and Grimella had not crept back, Moonshadow came out from the reeds. She stretched her wings and flew quietly over the pond. Now, where did the egg fall?

Moonshadow fluttered backwards and forwards over the water, but there was no sign of the dragon's egg.

'I'll have to use some fairy dust,' she said to herself. She rubbed her fingers together and tiny sparkles of light twinkled over her hands. It was like they were coated in fine gold dust. Moonshadow blew the golden fairy dust from her hands.

It floated on the pond. The moon shining on the water made the fairy dust shimmer. Then, the fairy dust started to sink and fade, except for one place. It was there that the dust settled on a round, egg-shaped object glowing brightly. Moonshadow gasped with delight when she saw the dragon's egg.

'Hmm. It's in rather a deep place,' she said, hovering over the spot where the dragon's egg was shining.

As Moonshadow stared at the water, a few ripples disturbed the surface. There was a silvery flash under the water and then someone whispered, 'Hello Moonshadow, what are you doing here? It's very late and you should be at home, fast asleep.'

'Oh! Hi Pearl. I'm so glad to see you,' whispered Moonshadow. 'A mermaid is just what I need.'

Pearl smiled. Her tail flapped gently up and down in the water, and her wet, rainbow-coloured hair floated around her. She was pleased to see her friend.

'See that glowing object at the bottom of the pond?' said Moonshadow quietly.

'It's a dragon's egg. I need to get it out of the water and hide it.'

Pearl ducked her head under the water and swam deep down to examine the egg.

When she popped back up again, she said, 'It's very large. Why do you need to hide it, Moonshadow? Is it yours to take?'

'No, it isn't mine to take, but then, it isn't Grimella's either.'

Pearl took a deep breath when she heard the witch's name and asked, 'Does

18

she want it for making powerful magic spells?'

'Yes,' replied Moonshadow.

As Pearl looked back down at the dragon's egg, her wet hair shone in the moonlight.

'I'll help you to hide it. It won't be good to have a witch using a dragon's egg for more powerful magic. What do you want me to do?'

Moonshadow looked thoughtful for a moment. The size of the dragon's egg might be too much for Pearl to carry all the way from the bottom of the pond to the top.

'Can you see any long strands of pondweed?' she asked Pearl.

'Yes, there's plenty just over there in the deeper part of the pond,' said the mermaid.

'Good. Gather as much as you can and tie it together to make one long piece. Then wrap one end around the egg and give the other end to me.'

Pearl flicked her tail and disappeared into the water.

From time to time, Moonshadow caught a silvery glimpse of Pearl's tail as she twisted and turned in and out of the pondweed. Pearl tied the weed together, before wrapping it around the dragon's egg and giving the other end to Moonshadow.

'Right, when you start to lift the egg, I'll help by pulling the pondweed gently up towards the edge of the pond. We should be able to roll the egg out of the water and find somewhere where we can hide it,' whispered Moonshadow.

When Pearl began lifting the dragon's

egg, Moonshadow started to pull gently. She didn't know how fragile the egg was and didn't want to break it. Slowly, the egg was brought up to the surface, and

Pearl carefully pushed the egg towards Moonshadow.

When the egg was at the edge of the pond, she fluttered over Pearl's head and reached down to help the mermaid roll the egg onto the damp mud.

'That's as much as I can do,' panted Pearl.

'Thank you, Pearl. I couldn't have done it without you,' said Moonshadow, as she removed some pondweed from the dragon egg. Afterwards, she bent down and gave Pearl a hug. A small shower of fairy dust fell onto Pearl's hair and glittered like tiny, golden stars.

Pearl was just about to swim away when she felt Moonshadow's arms tighten.

'What's the matter?' asked Pearl with alarm. 'Is there a witch about?'

Moonshadow shook her head. 'No… look at the egg!'

Pearl glanced at the muddy bank. The egg was glowing. It started with a light yellow glow, which then deepened to orange.

'What's happening?' Pearl asked.

Her arms trembled and Moonshadow knew that the mermaid was afraid. She was too, but she wasn't going to fly away and leave her friend.

The egg began changing colour again, from orange to a deep ruby red. Then, there was a little sound of cracking as the egg began to hatch.

Chapter 4

Both Moonshadow and Pearl watched as the dragon's egg cracked more and more. Bits of shell broke away and fell onto the mud. A small nose poked out of one side.

Soon, a head appeared. Then, the baby dragon wiggled its head to make the hole larger, but after struggling for ten minutes, it began to make a whimpering sound.

'I think it's stuck,' said Moonshadow. 'It's crying because it can't get out. For such a large egg, that dragon is rather small. I think it's hatched too early.'

'I think you're right,' agreed Pearl. 'What are we going to do?'

'Help it, of course,' said Moonshadow, flying to the egg. She began to pull the eggshell apart. Her hands touched the dragon's head. She expected it to feel hard and scaly, but it wasn't; instead, it was soft and delicate. The dragon lifted its head and mewed like a new-born kitten.

'What does it look like?' asked Pearl, trying to lift herself up out of the water as far as she could to see the dragon.

Moonshadow broke away some more shell and a little paw moved as the dragon sensed she was trying to help it.

'It's adorable,' she told Pearl.

The mermaid waited and finally, enough eggshell was removed for the dragon to escape. It wobbled towards the pond. Moonshadow rushed after it, afraid that it would fall in, but it just lay down and lapped up some water. Pearl swam slowly towards the dragon. She didn't want to frighten it.

Moonshadow was right; the dragon was so cute that Pearl wanted to cuddle it.

Instead, she carefully put out her hand to stroke it.

Like Moonshadow, she was surprised to find that it was soft.

'Its scales aren't hard, and it's white all over,' she said, as the dragon gazed at her and gave a tiny mew. 'Moonshadow, how are you going to hide a baby dragon? It's going to be more difficult than hiding an egg,' she asked.

Moonshadow looked worried.

'I know, but not only that, if it's going to live, I need to find out what it eats, as well as finding a way of moving it from this place. It can't fly yet and it's too weak to walk any distance.'

'I've got a large seashell at home. It would make a nice cradle,' offered Pearl. 'Do you want me to go and fetch it?'

'That's a good idea, thank you, Pearl.' Pearl dived under the water. A stream of bubbles rose to the surface – the only sign that she had been there at all.

Chapter 5

Pearl was only gone for a few minutes, but to Moonshadow, it felt like hours. She sat down by the dragon and was surprised when it crawled onto her lap. Moonshadow kept watch, just in case an owl flew overhead and decided that a baby dragon would make a tasty meal. When Pearl returned, she was pushing a rounded seashell over the surface of the pond. The baby dragon had fallen asleep on Moonshadow's lap, so she had to gently move it to one side so that she could pull the shell from the water. After tipping out any water from the inside, Moonshadow looked for some soft moss to make a bed for the dragon to lie on. Pearl waited by the dragon to make sure it stayed safe.

'I think the moss looks quite comfortable,' said Moonshadow, as she patted it down into the shell. 'Pearl, can you wake the dragon for me please?' she asked.

Pearl leaned towards the dragon's ears and started to sing a mermaid song. The dragon's eyes opened. It saw the seashell, mewed, crawled onto the moss and snuggled down.

Moonshadow gathered some dried reeds and wound them around the shell, to enable her to pull it along behind her.

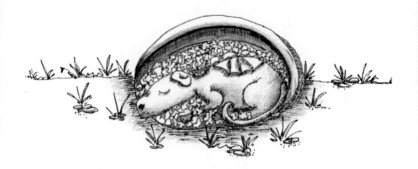

'I'll have to take the dragon home with me and keep it there, so I'd better get going,' said Moonshadow. 'I don't know how long this will take, even with using fairy magic.'

Pearl floated on her back and watched Moonshadow rub her hands together to create fairy dust. She sprinkled it around and under the shell. Pearl was amazed when the seashell gained hundreds of teeny wings, all fluttering madly to get the shell airborne. Moonshadow took the reeds in her hands, opened her wings, and flew up to the sky. But she found, even with magic, that towing the baby dragon in the seashell was hard work.

'Bye Moonshadow,' called Pearl quietly. 'Let me know how you get on...'

She felt sad that the cute, frail dragon had gone. Suddenly, she felt lonely without her friend, so she slid gracefully under the water to find a rock where she could sit in the moonlight and sing her mermaid songs.

Chapter 6

Moonshadow grew quite breathless, as she flew along, pulling the seashell behind her. On the way home, she had stopped several times when she heard an owl hooting.

Normally, when she was out on a full moon night, she could hide if an owl soared overhead. But tonight was different. Moonshadow was terrified that an owl might swoop down and steal the helpless baby dragon.

At last, she reached her little room inside the oak tree, where she lived alone. The small wings on the seashell gently lowered it to the floor. The fluttering stopped and the little wings vanished. The baby dragon had slept peacefully all the way home.

Moonshadow opened a cupboard and took out a quilt, stuffed with dandelion seed fluff. She covered the dragon and, because she was so tired, she pulled back the flower petals on her own bed, crawled in, and fell into a deep sleep.

The fairy felt like she had only just closed her eyes when she was woken by a loud banging and shouting at her front door.

'Moonshadow! Moonshadow! Open the door!'

It sounded like Willow's voice.

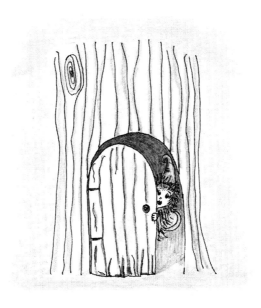

Moonshadow opened the door carefully, just to make sure it really was Willow. The sunshine streamed in and Moonshadow blinked at the brightness.

'I'm so glad you're here,' said Willow quietly. 'Apparently, last night, a fairy stole and broke a dragon's egg. This morning, Grimella, the witch, visited our Woodland Queen and told her she had found fairy dust by the broken egg. The witch demanded to know the name of the fairy who had

committed the crime.' Willow paused. 'The Queen told Grimella that it wasn't any of her fairies and to go away. Moonshadow,'

Willow paused again, 'you went out for the full moon last night…'

Moonshadow wearily opened the door and said, 'You'd better come in.'

Willow froze when she saw the baby dragon, sitting on a bed of moss in the seashell.

'Oh Moonshadow! What have you done?' she cried.

Chapter 7

'I didn't steal the egg,' Moonshadow protested, and she explained to Willow that it was Grimella and her bat that were responsible for taking the dragon's egg.

'But why didn't you leave it at the bottom of the pond?' asked Willow. 'You should have been in bed, not visiting the pond. Moonshadow, you really had no business taking something that didn't belong to you.'

'Pooh!' replied Moonshadow sulkily. 'Pearl agreed with me that letting a witch have a dragon's egg for making more powerful magic was not a good idea. She helped me to get the egg out of the pond.'

Willow became thoughtful. Pearl was a good mermaid, and if she had agreed with Moonshadow then maybe they had done the right thing.

'Anyway, the egg started to hatch, but the dragon got stuck. It was so helpless that I had to do something,' grumbled Moonshadow, 'and once it was out of the egg, it was so weak that an owl would have easily caught it. I couldn't leave the baby dragon to fend for itself,' she said.

Moonshadow looked rather unhappy.

Willow nodded in agreement. 'Of course not. The question is what are we going to do now?'

Moonshadow noticed that Willow had said 'what are *we* going to do now', and she started to feel happier because her friend was going to help her.

The baby dragon mewed a pitiful sound. Willow went over to the seashell and said, 'Aww! It's so cute. What shall we call it? It's so white, as white as a snowflake,' Willow said, and smiled. 'Snowflake,' she repeated, 'that's a good name – we'll call it Snowflake.'

Moonshadow was startled at the suggestion of giving the baby dragon a name. Willow stretched out her hand to stroke Snowflake. The dragon blinked, yawned and made a smacking noise with its lips.

'Have you fed Snowflake?'

'What?'

A shiver of panic crept up Moonshadow's spine and spread into her wings.

'I don't know what a baby dragon eats,' she muttered.

'It's called Snowflake!' Willow insisted. 'And I read somewhere that they like wild milk-berries.'

'I think I know where I can find some,' said Moonshadow, picking up a basket made of woven twigs.

'You stay here and look after Snowflake. I'll be as quick as I can.'

Moonshadow put the basket over her arm and flew down from her oak tree.

Chapter 8

There was a small glade in the woodland where the milk-berries grew, but there was a problem. Before Moonshadow could reach the glade, she had to pass the Great Oak, and who lived in the Great Oak? The Woodland Queen who Grimella had visited this morning!

Although the Woodland Queen told the witch it wasn't any of her fairies that had stolen the dragon's egg, if she saw Moonshadow, there was a risk she might start asking questions. A few weeks ago, the Queen had reminded everyone of the dangers of being out after sunset. She had looked directly at Moonshadow. Did the Queen suspect that she went out to play in the moonlight?

Moonshadow flitted behind tree trunks, ferns and shrubs. Outside the Great Oak, there were elves, pixies and fairies, all busy with their daily chores. There was a queue at the bakery, where the smell of chestnut bread and beechnut pancakes filled the air. At the grocery store, the shopkeeper was putting out baskets of fresh mushrooms and rosehips. Moonshadow crept behind a gorse bush and watched. Next, she swiftly moved to a large blackberry patch. She looked about and moved further away until finally, she was far enough away from the Great Oak to fly to the glade beyond.

She quickly found the milk-berries and filled her basket with the small, white fruits.

All the time she picked the fruit, she was thinking about the dragon. How much did it eat? How would she manage to keep getting enough food as it grew larger and larger? Where would she keep it when it was too big for her room? As well as, what would happen when the Woodland Queen found out that she had been the fairy who had taken the egg, even if it was for a good reason? And all this because, as Willow told her, she should have been asleep in bed and not visiting the pond!

Moonshadow lifted the basket onto her arm and headed for home. A dark shadow blocked out the sun for a few seconds, then, there was a rush of wind, followed by a terrifying roar.

Moonshadow fled to the ground and looked up. She saw an enormous, white dragon flying overhead, and it was heading straight for the Great Oak!

Chapter 9

'Oh no!' cried Moonshadow. Her wings buzzed as she flew back to the Great Oak. She heard another deafening dragon roar. There were also other sounds of shouting and crying. Moonshadow heard them as she drew closer to the Great Oak. Fairies were flying in all directions, and elves and pixies were scattering into the undergrowth.

Moonshadow held her breath and hid behind the gorse bush once more. The large, white dragon descended and landed by the Great Oak. Moonshadow watched the Woodland Queen emerge and stand on her wooden balcony, high up in the oak tree.

The Queen wore her cloth of woodland-green robes and carried her witch-hazel staff; her hair, which was the colour of autumn leaves, flowed around her, as she stood looking down at the white dragon. The white dragon bowed its head.

'You are the dragon mother whose egg has been stolen?' asked the Queen. She was beginning to feel annoyed. This morning, Grimella had made an unpleasant scene, and now, there was an enormous dragon causing disruption amongst the woodland.

The dragon nodded.

'A witch told me that last night, a fairy stole a dragon's egg and broke it. I said it was *not* one of my fairies.' The Queen paused, and then said, 'I'm sorry, that is all I know.'

She hoped the dragon would leave quickly so that everything would settle down again. The white dragon moaned and hung its head low to the ground. Even from where Moonshadow was hiding, she could see large tears trickling down the dragon's scaly nose. She felt terrible, and before she stopped to think about it, she rushed out from the gorse bush and flew to the white dragon.

'Please don't cry,' Moonshadow begged, 'your baby is quite safe.'

'MOONSHADOW!'

The fairy turned around slowly and looked up at the Woodland Queen.

'WHAT HAVE YOU BEEN UP TO THIS TIME?'

The white dragon lifted her head and studied Moonshadow. The dragon's tears stopped and there was hope in her eyes.

Moonshadow curtsied to the Queen and kept her eyes cast down towards the ground. She explained all that had happened.

Although Moonshadow spoke clearly, the Queen heard the tremble in the fairy's voice. She frowned. This fairy was one who did not like keeping to the rules.

'And is the baby dragon still at your place?' asked the Queen, in a frosty voice.

'Yes, Your Majesty. I was just on my way home to give it some milk-berries. It's so hungry,' replied Moonshadow, pointing to the basket for the Queen to see.

'Well, feed it as fast as you can and then be good enough to bring it here and give it to this ice dragon,' ordered the Queen. She was anxious. An upset dragon was not a good thing to have waiting around.

Moonshadow glanced at the white dragon. So, it was an ice dragon – a dragon that breathed ice, not fire!

'Moonshadow, I'm extremely cross with you for being out at night when you should have been asleep in bed. You

56

know that I only warned everybody of the dangers again recently,' the Queen scolded.

Moonshadow's face grew hot.

'However, you *have* saved this dragon's baby. Now go and do as I have asked,' the Woodland Queen said, and then sighed. 'I really don't know what I'm going to do with you!'

Moonshadow curtsied again and flew swiftly back to her room in the oak tree.

Chapter 10

When Moonshadow entered her room, she heard Willow humming to the baby ice dragon.

'We can give Snowflake some food and then we must take it to the Great Oak,' Moonshadow told her friend.

Willow stopped humming and listened as Moonshadow told her why.

'Oh dear! The Queen sounds very cross,' mumbled Willow.

'Yes, but she also said that I did save the baby dragon, so maybe everything will be all right,' replied Moonshadow, trying to convince herself that it would all work out okay.

The dragon mewed. Willow took some milk-berries and offered them to the dragon. It sniffed, and then looked at Willow, as if expecting her to do something.

'Why isn't it eating them?' asked Moonshadow.

'Maybe it doesn't know how. I think we'll have to demonstrate,' said Willow.

'Do you mean… we have to eat the milk-berries? But there hasn't been a frost to make them sweet. They'll taste disgusting!' complained Moonshadow.

'What about chewing one up to soften it and then feeding it to Snowflake?' suggested Willow.

'Good idea! Here you go…' said Moonshadow quickly.

Willow took the berry and popped it into her mouth. Moonshadow watched as Willow's face puckered. Even so, she chewed the berry until it was soft, then removed it from her mouth and offered it to Snowflake. The dragon sniffed the mashed berry, opened its mouth and ate it.

'Well, that's good,' said Moonshadow.

'Yes, but the bad news is that all the berries will have to be chewed,' groaned Willow.

'Hurry up then, the Queen is waiting,' said Moonshadow.

'It would be much faster if you helped,' complained Willow.

'Oh, all right!'

Both the fairies began chewing up the berries. They screwed up their faces, as the sourness from the milk-berries stung their tongues and made their eyes water.

Snowflake gobbled the berries faster than Moonshadow and Willow could chew.

Chapter 11

When all the berries were gone, Snowflake yawned and lay down on the seashell bed once more. Moonshadow rubbed her hands and blew fairy dust around the seashell. Tiny wings appeared on the shell again and began fluttering. The shell rose into the air.

Willow opened the door, as Moonshadow picked up the reeds to help guide the shell out of the room and on towards the Great Oak.

As they approached the large tree, they saw that a large crowd had gathered. When Willow saw the ice dragon, she breathed in deeply. It was very large and one day, Snowflake would be like that too.

They guided the seashell down so that the ice dragon could see Snowflake. The baby was curious and peered out at everyone.

The Woodland Queen inclined her head to Moonshadow and said, 'After you left us, the ice dragon said there would be a reward for the safe return of her baby. As you are the one who saved it, is there anything you would like?'

Moonshadow became thoughtful, then asked the Queen in a low voice, 'May I have a snow party for everyone tonight?'

'Are you able to make a snow party?' the Woodland Queen asked, turning to the dragon.

The ice dragon looked pleased and nodded.

'Very well,' answered the Queen. 'I give special permission for all woodlanders to attend a snow party tonight from six o'clock until midnight, to be held at the pond where Moonshadow rescued the baby ice dragon. Please wear warm clothing.'

The cheers that went up deafened Moonshadow. Pixies and elves threw

their hats into the air; fairies squealed with excitement at the thought of going to a party at *night time*, and danced in a ring around Moonshadow and Willow.

'SILENCE PLEASE!' commanded the Queen. 'There are many preparations to be done. Who would like to help?'

Plenty of hands shot up into the air.

'Come with me,' said the Queen. She departed with a swish of her woodland-green robes, as all the helpers followed.

The ice dragon nudged Moonshadow gently. The fairy felt the rough dragon scales and wondered how soon Snowflake's scales would be like this. Willow stood next to Moonshadow.

'Should we tell the ice dragon what we called the baby?' she whispered.

'Don't you mean – what you called it?' replied Moonshadow, then, because she thought she had sounded unkind, she quickly added, 'Yes, we should, because Snowflake suits the baby dragon, and it would be strange to hear it called something else.'

Moonshadow cleared her throat. 'Ice dragon – I hope you don't mind, but we were thinking what sort of name suited your baby and we... er... rather liked Snowflake...'

Before Moonshadow could say anymore, the big dragon lifted her head,

opened her mouth and shot a blast of icy air into the clouds. A single snowflake floated down and landed on the baby ice dragon's nose.

'Snowflake it is,' purred the dragon.

Chapter 12

At six o'clock, Moonshadow arrived at the woodland pond. Fairies, elves and pixies were dressed in their warm winter clothes. They were all excited about being allowed to stay at a party that would go on after sunset!

When the woodland fairy folk saw Moonshadow, they all clapped. She looked around at the beautiful wintry scene before her. The ice dragon had been busy!

Moonshadow noticed that the pond was frozen solid and there were party tables on the ice. The tables were decorated with polka-dot cloths, and there were beeswax candles in ice candelabras, waiting to be lit when it grew dark.

Helpers brought out baskets filled with chestnut bread, as well as berries and nuts for everyone to have a delicious feast.

A gentle tinkling sound drifted towards Moonshadow, and she realised that it came from the hundreds of icicles hanging in the trees and bushes. The reeds and grasses at the pond edge were coated in twinkling frost, and snow covered the muddy banks like a clean sheet. The whole place was filled with magic and happiness.

'It's all so pretty,' gasped Moonshadow.

She picked up a handful of snow. 'I hope everyone has a lovely time!'

The Queen raised her witch-hazel staff and it became silent.

'Tonight, we thank the ice dragon for creating this winter wonderland for us to enjoy, especially as it's still summer,' she said. 'Also, thank you, Moonshadow, for choosing a reward that everyone can share, not just something for yourself. It proves you have a generous heart. Now, let the party begin!'

Chapter 13

Moonshadow gazed around, as the fairy folk started to sing and dance. Willow joined her. She pointed to a tree stump at the far edge of the pond, where Pearl was sitting. The mermaid waved at them and then continued stroking Snowflake, who was now sitting by her side. The snow crunched under Moonshadow's and Willow's boots, as they walked over to Pearl.

'Hello Pearl. Why are you looking after Snowflake?' asked Moonshadow, suddenly realising that the ice dragon wasn't there.

Pearl smiled, 'The ice dragon asked me to. She has to do something and will be back shortly.'

Moonshadow touched Snowflake's head, and she found that the dragon wasn't soft any more. Already, Snowflake was getting dragon scales, just like her mother.

Soon, the ice dragon returned. It swooped around the pond and landed by the tree stump. Moonshadow felt strange. Part of her was happy that Snowflake would now be with her mother, but another part of her felt sad; she had rescued the egg and seen it hatch; she had seen how cute the baby dragon was; she had taken it home and now, it was going away. She would miss Snowflake, and it also meant it was the end of her adventure.

The ice dragon approached Moonshadow and held out something small in its paw. The item glittered in the light.

'It's beautiful!' exclaimed Willow. 'Is it for Moonshadow?'

'Yes,' purred the dragon. 'I've looked after it for a very long time. But now, I have Snowflake to look after, so it's time to pass this on to someone else; someone I know I can trust. Who else, but the fairy that saved my baby?' she said.

Moonshadow took the offered item. It had seemed small in the dragon's paw, but now that she held it, it was very big.

'It looks like a very large diamond!' gasped Moonshadow. 'But look! There's something inside it!' She took a deep breath. 'It… it looks like a heart,' she whispered.

'It's the pink heart diamond,' replied the dragon. 'It's very precious and extremely important. It belonged to the ancient Queen of Amshir.' The dragon paused, and then said, 'I now make you the Guardian of the Pink Heart. You must guard it with your life.'

'But I've never heard of this ancient queen!' said Moonshadow, admiring the jewel.

'But you will, Moonshadow – one day, you will,' said the ice dragon, picking up Snowflake in her mouth. The ice dragon opened her wings and flapped upwards. Swirls of snowflakes blew across the pond. By the time the snowflakes had settled, the dragons were gone.

Willow took Moonshadow's arm and smiled. 'You do lead an exciting life,

Moonshadow,' she said, 'but what are you going to do with the diamond?'

Moonshadow sighed. 'I don't know. If I have to guard it with my life then I'll need to find a safe place to hide it.' She sighed again. 'For now though, I think we ought to enjoy the rest of the party. Pearl, can I leave the diamond with you for the moment?' she asked, holding out the pink heart diamond. 'I wouldn't want to drop it in the snow. I'd never find it in this beautiful, white, winter wonderland!'

'Of course you can. I won't be going home until the pond melts,' Pearl told her, and carefully took the diamond. Willow took Moonshadow's hand, but before they joined the snow party, something occurred to Moonshadow.

She turned around and said, 'Thank you, Pearl. I couldn't have rescued Snowflake without your help. This party is your reward too. Would you like me to bring you some party food?'

'Oh yes please, Moonshadow! I'd love to try the chestnut bread,' said Pearl, blushing and smiling.

Moonshadow and Willow walked over the frozen pond to the party tables. Tonight, at sunset, nobody had to go to bed. They would all stay up to party under the stars and the moon, and they would see why Moonshadow loved to play in its silvery light. It was going to be a wonderful night!

If you have enjoyed this book, please be kind enough to leave a review on Amazon. Thank you.

www.amazon.co.uk

Moonshadow will return in:
Book 2 – *Moonshadow and the Mystery of the Moonlight Painter*

If you would like to download a free copy of Angela's 45-page educational guide to Creative Writing for Kids, please go to her website:

www.angelajamesauthor.co.uk

Join Angela James on
Twitter: @AJames_author
And
Facebook:www.facebook.com/angelajamesauthor.co.uk

Acknowledgements

My thanks as always to
Leila, my Guiding Angel!

Extra Fairy Fun

The Baby Ice Dragon Poem

Moonshadow is a fairy,
who loves to play at night,
She goes out in secret,
to see the stars and moonlight.

One night she overhears a witch
and stays hidden in the reeds,
the witch wants a dragon's egg
to fulfil her ambitious needs.

The egg is dropped into the pond
by the witch's bat,
the witch is cross and goes away,
thinking that's the end of that!

Moonshadow uses fairy dust,
the dragon's egg is found,
deep below the water,
it's a shining golden mound.

85

A mermaid friend is on the scene,
to give a helping hand,
they need to get the dragon egg
safely on the land.

The dragon's egg is rescued,
but then it begins to glow,
followed by a cracking sound,
and Moonshadow thinks, 'Oh no!'

Soon a baby dragon is here,
what will Moonshadow do?
How will she look after it?
She doesn't have a clue.

Her mermaid friend brings a shell,
to take the dragon home
to Moonshadow's house in a tree,
where she lives all alone.

Another fairy friend, called Willow,
knocks on Moonshadow's door,
She gasps in horror when she sees
a dragon on the floor.

The baby dragon is rather cute,
and so very, very white,
and Willow begins to understand
the baby dragon's plight.

They call the dragon Snowflake,
and it mews to be fed.
Moonshadow must get milkberries,
so off to a glade she sped.

A white dragon flies overhead,
and lands at the Great Oak,
its roars and cries as it lands,
terrify the woodland folk.

The Woodland Queen, on her balcony,
sees the dragon mother below.
She doesn't want an upset dragon,
and hopes that it will go.

The Woodland Queen cannot help,
and the dragon begins to cry,
Moonshadow rushes to her aid,
and the Queen begins to sigh.

What has the fairy been up to now
to cause this dragon pain?
The Queen looks very cross when
she asks Moonshadow to explain.

Moonshadow must fetch the baby,
and give it to the mother,
then maybe the dragon will leave,
and save a lot of bother.

Moonshadow flies back home,
and Snowflake must be fed,
but having to chew the milkberries
fills Moonshadow with dread.

Moonshadow and Willow chew the berries,
Snowflake eats them with glee,
and when the baby has finished eating,
it's time to leave the tree.

They take the baby to the mother,
carried in the shell,
the dragon and the Queen are happy,
and everything ends well.

A snow party is Moonshadow's reward,
to be held at the pond tonight,
everything is frozen,
frost twinkles in the light.

Fairy folk are dancing,
but before the dragons go,
a diamond is given to Moonshadow,
there's something she needs to know.

The diamond belonged to an ancient queen,
it's now in Moonshadow's care,
then with open wings the dragon left,
carrying Snowflake through the air.

The party will go on until midnight,
all the woodland folk are there,
Moonshadow chose this reward
for everyone to share.

Other books by Angela James

The Golden Moonbeam
Book 1 in The Amshir Legacy
Suitable for ages 9+

The Theft of the Black Diamond
Book 2 in The Amshir Legacy
Suitable for ages 9+

A FREE 45 page Creative Writing guide for Kids (and parents)
Available only from Angela James' website
www.angelajamesauthor.co.uk

How to turn a Genie into a
Geniusin one move!
A Beginner's Guide to Creative
Writing for Kids
(and Parents!)

By Angela James

Some illustrations for you to copy or colour:

A photograph of the author's real Moonshadow and baby ice dragon, taken in a woodland, not far from where she lives.

Lightning Source UK Ltd.
Milton Keynes UK
UKOW02f0935271116
288607UK00001B/1/P